How Can We Use Energy?

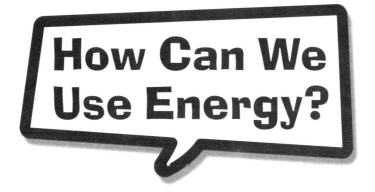

HOUGHTON MIFFLIN HARCOURT

PHOTOGRAPHY CREDITS: COVER g) ©Darryl Leniuk/Getty Images; 3 (t) ©Stephen O'Byrne/Flickr/Getty Images; 4 (r) ©Image Source/Getty Images; 5 (b) ©Darryl Leniuk/Getty Images; 7 (t) ©Michael T. Sedam/Corbis; 7 (b) ©Ashley Cooper/Corbis; 8 (b) ©VisitBritain/Britain On View/Getty Images; 9 (t) ©Kate Thompson/National Geographic/Getty Images; 12 (b) ©2006 Richard Megna/Fundamental Photographs; 13 (t) ©Liquidlibrary/Jupiterimages/Getty Images; 14 (b) ©Photodisc/Getty Images; 17 (r) ©C Squared Studios/PhotoDisc/Getty Images; 20 (b) ©Rob Lewine/Getty Images; 21 (t) ©Getty Images

Printed in Mexico

ISBN: 978-0-544-07338-8

10 0908 21 20 19 18 17

4500668768   A B C D E F G

Be an Active Reader!

Look for each word in yellow along with its meaning.

energy	thermal energy	conductor
kinetic energy	static electricity	insulator
potential energy	electric current	circuit
mechanical energy	chemical energy	parallel circuit
		series circuit

Underlined sentences answer the questions.

What is energy?

What are some different kinds of energy?

How can we measure and use thermal energy?

How can thermal energy move?

What makes up matter?

How do atoms affect electrical energy?

What are some conductors and insulators?

What are the parts of an electric circuit?

What kinds of circuits can electricity flow through?

How can energy change forms?

What is energy?

Lightning, headlights, and moving cars could not happen without energy.

Energy is the ability to cause changes in matter. You use energy every single day. Energy is what makes life on Earth possible. Without energy, there would be no movement and no sunlight. There would be no food, no sound, and no heat. There would also be no televisions or computers. Energy causes all of the changes that we can see or feel. There are different kinds of energy. Everything we see and do is a result of one of these kinds of energy. Let's learn about the different forms of energy.

What are some different kinds of energy?

The energy that an object has because of its movement is called kinetic energy. The energy that an object has because of its position or condition is potential energy. Position is where an object is. Condition is the state or quality of an object.

Before you move a skateboard on a downward slope, it has potential energy. When you push and move the skateboard, the potential energy changes to kinetic energy. Mechanical energy is the total potential and kinetic energy of an object. It is the total energy of the position and motion of an object.

Objects have potential energy when they are not moving. The energy changes to kinetic energy as the objects move.

What else happens when you push a skateboard? You can hear it and see it move. Light energy allows us to see, and sound energy allows us to hear.

Light travels in waves. It can move through space. It can pass through air and clear objects. When light energy bounces off objects, the light reaches our eyes so we can see the objects.

Sound energy is a kind of kinetic energy. Sounds are made when there are tiny movements, called vibrations, in matter. Sound vibrations move in waves through gases and liquids. They even move through solids. The vibrations move from an object to your ear. This is how you hear the sounds around you.

The skateboard wheels vibrate on the ground as they roll. This makes a sound.

How can we measure and use thermal energy?

All matter is made of tiny moving particles. The particles move quickly in an object that feels hot. The particles move much slower in an object that feels cold. Remember that kinetic energy is the energy of motion. That means moving particles have kinetic energy.

Thermal energy is the total amount of kinetic energy of the particles in a substance. An object has more thermal energy when it feels hot than when it feels cool.

Temperature is the measure of the average kinetic energy of the particles in a substance. We can measure an object's temperature with a tool called a thermometer. As an object gets hotter, the temperature increases. As an object gets colder, the temperature decreases.

We can measure temperature with a thermometer.

Earth has sources of thermal energy. Volcanoes contain rock so hot that it is melted. Geysers are springs with water that boils. The water becomes steam and shoots high into the air.

Thermal energy causes changes, just as other kinds of energy do. Thermal energy from the sun changes matter. Thermal energy can boil water. Thermal energy causes changes in food when it is cooked.

Thermal energy is also used in factories and industries. Thermal energy can make steam that turns fans called turbines. These turbines provide energy for machines that can produce electricity for our homes and businesses.

Volcanoes and geysers are the result of thermal energy deep underground.

A geothermal energy station changes thermal energy into other kinds of energy.

How can thermal energy move?

Heat is the energy that moves between objects of different temperatures. Heat moves from objects of higher temperatures to objects of lower temperatures. Heat is why your hand gets warm when you touch a hot cup of tea. The heat from the cup moves to your hand. The energy was transferred, or moved, from the cup to you.

The transfer of energy between particles that are in contact is called conduction. When you make a grilled cheese sandwich, you are using conduction. The pan and the bread are touching. As the temperature of the pan rises, the temperature of the sandwich also rises. The heat moves from one object to another.

The heat from the cup moves to the child's hands. His hands become warm.

Radiation transfers heat from the fire to the person's hands without touching.

Conduction happens when objects touch. Another process, called convection, can also transfer heat. Convection is the transfer of energy by currents in a liquid or a gas. Wind currents transferring heat are an example of how convection works. Convection also transfers heat through the water in a pot on the stove. The warmer water moves upward and the cooler water sinks, making a current. The cooler water is then heated again at the bottom.

Radiation is another way that energy is transferred. Radiation is the transfer of energy in waves without matter to carry it. Heat is transferred from the sun to Earth by radiation. When you hold out your hands near a campfire, your hands warm up because of radiation.

What makes up matter?

Matter is made up of tiny particles. These tiny pieces of matter are called atoms. They are so small that you cannot even see them. Atoms are made of even smaller parts called protons, neutrons, and electrons. Two of these parts have electric charges. A proton has a positive charge. An electron has a negative charge. A neutron is neutral, which means it has no charge.

Look at the diagram of an atom. The protons and neutrons are together in the center of the atom. This area is called the nucleus. The electrons move around in the space outside the nucleus.

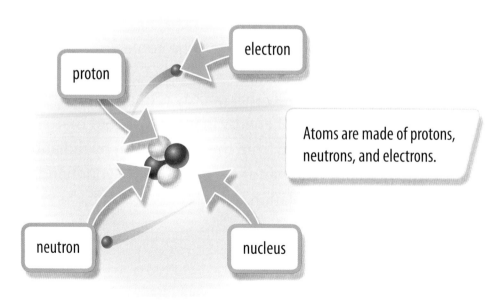

electron

proton

Atoms are made of protons, neutrons, and electrons.

neutron

nucleus

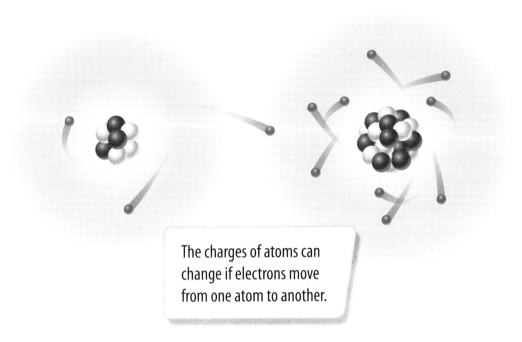

The charges of atoms can change if electrons move from one atom to another.

Protons and neutrons have electric charges. An atom with the same number of protons and neutrons has no charge. That's because it has an equal number of positive and negative charges. Atoms can gain or lose electrons. This may happen when the atoms bump into other atoms. The overall electric charge of an atom can change when this happens. Suppose a neutral atom loses an electron. The atom will then have a positive electric charge. Suppose a neutral atom gains an electron. The atom will then have a negative electric charge.

How do atoms affect electrical energy?

The movement of electric charges causes electrical energy. Particles with opposite charges attract each other. Particles with like charges push away from each other. Electrons can move from one object to another. When this happens, electric charges build up on the objects. The buildup of electric charges on an object is called static electricity. You may have felt the result of static electricity that is discharged. Have you ever touched a doorknob and got a shock? You feel a shock when the electrons move from your hand to the doorknob. You feel the energy from the electrons. Electric charges can build up in a clothes dryer, too. Clothes may stick together when charges build up.

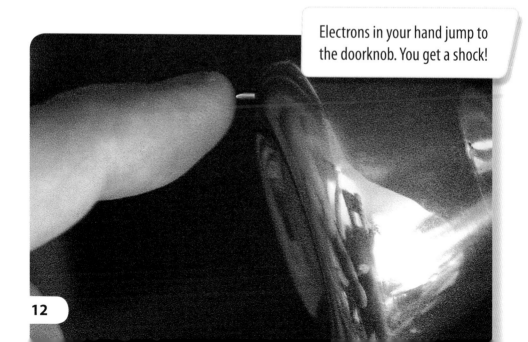

Electrons in your hand jump to the doorknob. You get a shock!

Electric charges can move in a fixed path, too. Electric current is the flow of electric charges along a path. You use electric current in your home and school. Electric current flows through wires. At home the electric current provides energy for our lights, toasters, televisions, and many other devices.

A flashlight's energy source is a battery.

Electrical energy in our homes comes from large energy stations that generate, or produce, the energy. The energy is made by changing other kinds of energy into electricity.

Many things that we use rely on electricity from batteries. Batteries use chemical energy, energy that is stored in matter and that can be released by a chemical reaction.

The energy to light the lamp comes from an energy station. It produces the electrical energy used by homes and businesses.

What are some conductors and insulators?

Electrical energy can be dangerous. Using it means we need specific materials. Some materials block the flow of electric charges. Other materials allow electric charges to flow better.

A conductor is a material that allows electricity to flow easily. Metals such as copper are good conductors of electricity. Many electrical wires are made out of copper. The charges can move easily and quickly along the wires.

Touching a wire with electric current flowing through it is very dangerous. That's why wires are covered with an insulator. An insulator is a material that prevents the flow of electricity.

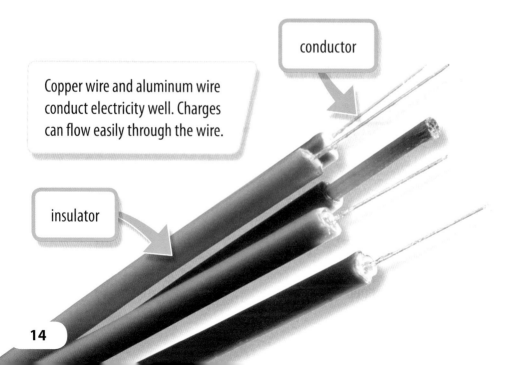

conductor

Copper wire and aluminum wire conduct electricity well. Charges can flow easily through the wire.

insulator

Rubber and plastics are good insulators. Electrical wires are covered in a coating of thick plastic. The plastic blocks the flow of electrons so that the electricity cannot flow out of the wire. This makes the wire safe. The plugs and outlets are also covered in insulators. Other materials also block the flow of electric charges. Glass, wood, and concrete are good insulators.

Staying safe around electricity is important. Electric shocks can be very strong. They can harm and even kill humans and animals. Electric discharges can cause fires. Insulators help us to use electricity safely.

The copper wire is covered in plastic. This insulates the flow of electricity.

A bulb, wires, and a battery are used to make a simple electric circuit.

What are the parts of an electric circuit?

A circuit is a complete path through which electric current can flow. Suppose you want to make a light bulb light up. You can make an electric circuit yourself, with adult supervision. You need a bulb, two wires, and an energy source. A common energy source is a battery. Energy is stored in a battery.

The copper wire should be covered in insulation, except at the ends. Touch the bare tip of a wire to the top of the metal part of the battery. Connect the other bare tip of the wire to the bottom of the light bulb. Then connect the other wire between the metal, mid-section of the bulb and the bottom end of the battery. The circuit will work only when all of these pieces are connected.

A lamp or light in your home has one more part to its circuit. It has a switch that lets the light be turned on and off. The switch stops and starts the flow of charged particles. It closes the circuit and allows electricity to flow when it is on.

A closed circuit is a circuit in which electricity flows in a complete loop. There are no breaks in the circuit to make the charges stop flowing. Any switch in the circuit is closed so that charges can pass. An open circuit is a circuit in which there is an opening. Any switch is turned off and the charges cannot flow.

When you turn off a light in your home, you change a closed circuit to an open circuit. A bulb will only light in a closed circuit.

What kinds of circuits can electricity flow through?

Electricity in our homes works a little differently from a circuit you make on your own. Electricity comes from huge energy stations instead of a battery. The electricity goes along wires to cities and towns. Then it goes to homes and other buildings. Finally, it goes throughout rooms in a building. Electricity flows through many wires. These connection points allow us to turn some connections on while others are off.

A parallel circuit is an electric circuit that has more than one path for the electric charges to follow. These are the kinds of circuits found in a home. You can turn off a kitchen light while the refrigerator is still running. You can watch a television show in the living room with different lights on.

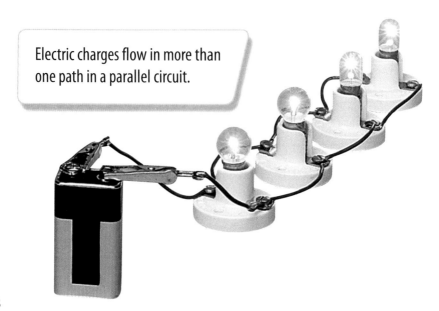

Electric charges flow in more than one path in a parallel circuit.

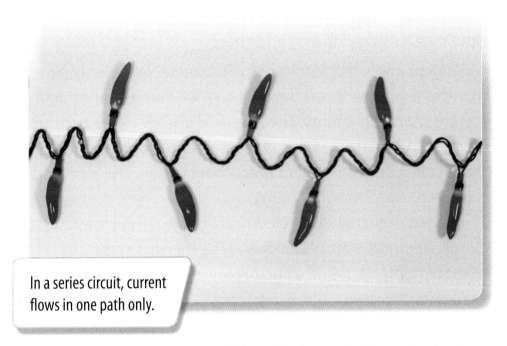

In a series circuit, current flows in one path only.

A parallel circuit is a useful kind of circuit. If one device is not working, the rest of the devices can still work. This is not the case with another kind of circuit, the series circuit. A series circuit is an electric circuit in which electric charges have only one path to follow. There may be many light bulbs or other electrical devices along that path. Some party lights are made this way. If one bulb does not work, the rest of the lights will not work, either.

How can energy change forms?

Did you know that energy can't be made? It can only be changed from one form to another. When you use a flashlight, you are changing energy. The chemical energy in the battery changes to electrical energy. As that energy flows through the circuit, a bulb lights. This is another change. The electrical energy changed to light energy.

You can use changes in electrical energy to do many things. Electrical energy can change to thermal energy to heat our homes. It can change to sound energy to play music.

Electrical energy can be changed to sound and light energy.

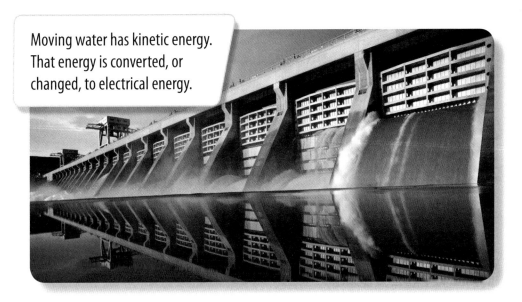

Moving water has kinetic energy. That energy is converted, or changed, to electrical energy.

An electrical energy station converts large amounts of energy. Some electrical energy stations change mechanical energy into electrical energy. For example, flowing water from dams can make turbines work. Thermal energy can also be changed to electrical energy. The electricity is then sent to homes and businesses. There it is changed into other forms of energy that we need and use every day. We may change it back to thermal energy when we cook. We may change it to light and sound energy when we watch television.

Make a Circuit

You can make an electric circuit with the help of an adult. Remember to work safely and use covered wires. Use a D-cell battery, two wires, and a small light bulb to put the circuit together. Follow the instructions on page 16. Talk about the difference between when the circuit is open and when the circuit is closed.

Keep an Energy Log

Explain how you use different kinds of energy during one day. In a notebook, write down things that you do, and explain what kind of energy each activity uses. Are there times when different kinds of energy are being used at the same time? Report your findings to the class.

Glossary

chemical energy [KEM·ih·kuhl EN·er·jee] Energy that can be released by a chemical reaction. *A battery stores chemical energy.*

circuit [SER·kit] A path along which electric charges can flow. *A circuit is closed when electricity flows through it.*

conductor [kuhn·DUK·ter] A material that lets heat or electricity travel through it easily. *Copper is a good conductor of electricity.*

electric current [ee·LEK·trik KER·uhnt] The flow of electric charges along a path. *Electric current is used to light a lamp.*

energy [EN·er·jee] The ability to cause changes in matter. *We use energy to do everything in our lives.*

insulator [IN·suh·layt·er] A material that does not let heat or electricity move through it easily. *Rubber is a good insulator of electric charges.*

kinetic energy [kih·NET·ik EN·er·jee] The energy an object has because of motion. *A bouncing ball has kinetic energy.*

mechanical energy [muh·KAN·ih·kuhl EN·er·jee] The total potential and kinetic energy of an object. *A moving car has mechanical energy.*

Glossary

parallel circuit [PAIR•uh•lel SER•kit] An electric circuit that has more than one path for the electric charges to flow. *A school's electricity flows in a parallel circuit.*

potential energy [poh•TEN•shuhl EN•er•jee] Energy that an object has because of its position or its condition. *When a ball is not rolling or bouncing, it has potential energy.*

series circuit [SEER•eez SER•kit] An electric circuit in which the electric charges have only one path to follow. *Some party lights are arranged in a series circuit.*

static electricity [STAT•ik ee•lek•TRIS•ih•tee] The buildup of electric charges on an object. *Lightning is caused by static electricity.*

thermal energy [THUHR•mul EN•er•jee] The total amount of kinetic energy of the particles in a substance. *A hot object has a lot of thermal energy.*